DAREDEVIL SPORTS

CAVE DIVING

By Hal Garrison

HOT TOPICS

Gareth Stevens PUBLISHING

Please visit our website, www.garethstevens.com. For a free color catalog of all our high-quality books, call toll free 1-800-542-2595 or fax 1-877-542-2596.

Library of Congress Cataloging-in-Publication Data

Names: Garrison, Hal, author.
Title: Cave diving / Hal Garrison.
Description: New York : Gareth Stevens Publishing, [2018] | Series: Daredevil Sports | Includes index.
Identifiers: LCCN 2017032562| ISBN 9781538211151 (Library bound) | ISBN 9781538211137 (Paperback) | ISBN 9781538211144 (6 pack)
Subjects: LCSH: Cave diving--Juvenile literature. | Outdoor recreation--Juvenile literature.
Classification: LCC GV200.63 .G37 2018 | DDC 796.52/5--dc23
LC record available at https://lccn.loc.gov/2017032562

Published in 2018 by
Gareth Stevens Publishing
111 East 14th Street, Suite 349
New York, NY 10003

Designer: Bethany Perl
Editor: Kate Mikoley

Photo credits: Cover, pp. 1 (diver), 20, 27 Reinhard Dirscherl/ullstein bild/Getty Images; pp. 2-32 (background) gumbao/Shutterstock.com; pp. 4, 7 littlesam/Shutterstock.com; pp. 5, 17, 29 Martyn Farr/Barcroft Media/Getty Images; p. 8 Angelo Giampiccolo/Shutterstock.com; p. 9 Marcus Bay/Shutterstock.com; pp. 11, 23, 25 Victor Lyagushk/Barcroft Media/Getty Images; p. 13 DAAgius/Shutterstock.com; p. 14 Ethan Daniels/Shutterstock.com; pp. 15, 22 divedog/Shutterstock.com; p. 19 sergemi/Shutterstock.com; p. 21 Microgen/Shutterstock.com; p. 26 timsimages/Shutterstock.com.

Printed in the United States of America

CPSIA compliance information: Batch #CW18GS: For further information contact Gareth Stevens, New York, New York at 1-800-542-2595.

CONTENTS

UNDERWATER EXPLORATION

Deep in the sea, a diver swims through a space not much bigger than herself. Sunlight doesn't reach here, so the diver wears her own light. Plants and many animals can't live here, but there's still much to **explore**.

RISK FACTOR

Highly trained cave divers have explored hundreds of feet below the surface, or top, of the ocean. However, many suggest not going below 130 feet (40 m) because the change in pressure can be harmful.

Cave diving is a type of diving in which divers swim into underwater caves. Other kinds of diving include open-water diving and **cavern** diving. All divers need to learn how to open-water dive before they can cave dive.

RISK FACTOR

Open-water diving means the diver can swim directly up to reach the surface of the water and can see sunlight.

OPEN-WATER DIVERS

CAVING AND DIVING

"Caving" is a word used to describe the activity of exploring caves, usually above the water. Once people found caves below the water, they were interested in exploring those as well. Cave diving combines caving with underwater diving.

RISK FACTOR

Like regular cave explorers, cave divers often look for fossils and other things that could teach them more about Earth.

THE RIGHT GEAR

Cave divers enjoy views that most people won't see in their entire lifetime. The sights are beautiful. However, it can also be dangerous, or unsafe. Divers need to be trained and know how to use the right gear.

RISK FACTOR

The water in caves is often clearer than open water, making it easier for divers to view the sights around them.

Most divers use **scuba** gear to breathe and stay safe underwater. This includes a tank with a supply of air or gas to breathe and a mouthpiece to take it in. Most cave divers bring at least two tanks on every dive.

RISK FACTOR

Open-water divers commonly wear tanks on their back, but cave divers often wear them on their sides so they can fit into small openings.

The gas in a breathing tank is made up of a combination of different gases, including oxygen. You need oxygen to live. However, depending on how deep in the water you are, too much or too little of it could kill you!

RISK FACTOR

Too much oxygen can be toxic in deep water, so divers who are going deep sometimes need to change the mix of gases they're using.

IN THE DARK

When a diver goes into a cave, any light from the sun disappears. The inside of the cave is pitch black. That's why cave divers bring their own lights. These look like flashlights and are commonly worn on top of the hand. Some divers wear helmets with lights, too.

RISK FACTOR

Divers should bring at least two extra lights in case the one they're using goes out.

KEEPING SAFE

Cave divers need a lot of gear to stay safe, but bringing too much could be dangerous. Extra gear is important in case something breaks. However, unnecessary items could slow the diver down, or worse yet—get them stuck!

RISK FACTOR

Cave divers wear their gear in certain ways so they can move something, such as a breathing tank, out of the way if needed.

Swimming underwater for a long time can sometimes cause your body temperature to get very cold. This can be very unsafe and possibly deadly. To stop this from happening, cave divers often wear special suits that keep their body dry or warm.

RISK FACTOR

Cave divers also wear special fins and masks made to help them move smoothly and see well in the water.

Many underwater caves are like mazes, with lots of twists and turns. This can make it hard to find the way out. For this reason, divers use ropes as guides, called guidelines, which help them make their way back out of the cave.

RISK FACTOR

White is a popular color for guidelines because it's very reflective and easy to spot.

A RISKY ACTIVITY

Cave diving can provide beautiful views of things few people have seen. However, it can also be dangerous. If something goes wrong, it may be a long way out of the cave and up to the surface. Even skilled divers have died cave diving.

RISK FACTOR

Divers should leave two-thirds of their breathing gas for their trip out of the cave.

Not everyone can cave dive. Many skilled scuba divers don't even have what it takes to become a cave diver. Cave divers need to be very healthy and in excellent shape. They need years of training and special **certifications**.

RISK FACTOR

Successful divers commonly make more than 100 regular dives before becoming a cave diver!

SCIENCE IN THE CAVES

Many people love cave diving, but for others, it's more than just a fun activity—it's their job! Scientists are exploring underwater caves to learn more about our planet and the creatures that have lived on it.

RISK FACTOR

Some scientists even think their findings in underwater caves could help them learn about life on other planets!

SAFETY TIPS

ALL CAVE DIVERS SHOULD:

- have completed at least 100 regular dives.
- have proper training and certifications.
- bring at least three sources of light.
- stay within the suggested depths for their breathing tanks.
- save two-thirds of their gas for exiting the cave.
- use a guideline so they can find the exit of the cave.

FOR MORE INFORMATION

BOOKS

Hamilton, S. L. *Caving*. Minneapolis, MN: ABDO Publishing, 2014.

Loh-Hagan, Virginia. *Extreme Cave Diving*. Ann Arbor, MI: Cherry Lake Publishing, 2016.

Teitelbaum, Michael. *Scuba Diving*. Mankato, MN: The Child's World, 2012.

WEBSITES

The Cave Diving Website

www.cavediving.com

This site, run by a real cave diver, has answers to many questions you might have about this sport.

SCUBA Facts

kidskonnect.com/sports/scuba

Read more about scuba diving, an activity that helped form cave diving, here.

GLOSSARY

cavern: much like a cave, but the entrance and light from the sun can always be seen

certification: official approval to do something

explore: to search in order to find out new things

fossil: the hardened marks or remains of plants and animals that formed over thousands or millions of years

pressure: a force that pushes on something else

reflective: giving back light

scuba: a tool used for breathing while swimming underwater

INDEX